Mary
the Sharing
Fairy

To Darcie Horne

Special thanks to Rachel Elliot

Copyright © 2016 by Rainbow Magic Limited.

All rights reserved. Published by Scholastic Inc., *Publishers since 1920.* SCHOLASTIC and associated logos are trademarks and/or registered trademarks of Scholastic Inc. RAINBOW MAGIC is a trademark of Rainbow Magic Limited. Reg. U.S. Patent & Trademark Office and other countries. HIT and the HIT logo are trademarks of HIT Entertainment Limited.

The publisher does not have any control over and does not assume any responsibility for author or third-party websites or their content.

This book is a work of fiction. Names, characters, places, and incidents are either the product of the author's imagination or are used fictitiously, and any resemblance to actual persons, living or dead, business establishments, events, or locales is entirely coincidental.

ISBN 978-1-338-15768-0

10 9 8 7 6 5 4 3 2 1   17 18 19 20 21

Printed in the U.S.A.   40
First edition, July 2017

Mary the Sharing Fairy

by Daisy Meadows

SCHOLASTIC INC.

Jack Frost's Ice Castle

Rainspell Island

The Friendship Fairies like big smiles.
They want to spread good cheer for miles.
Those pests want people to connect,
And treat one another with respect.

I don't agree! I just don't care!
I want them all to feel despair.
And when their charms belong to me,
Each friend will be an enemy!

Contents

Painting Plans

"I can't wait to find out what we'll be doing at the Summer Friends Camp today," said Kirsty Tate.

She grinned at her best friend, Rachel Walker, who was bouncing up and down on a hoppity hop. They were inside a brightly colored tent in Rainspell Park, where the vacation day camp was based.

"Whatever it is, I'm sure it'll be fun," said Rachel, her blond curls flying around her head as she bounced. "We'll be together!"

Rachel and Kirsty had been friends ever since their first meeting on Rainspell Island. It was an extra-special place for them because they had also become friends with the fairies during that first visit.

This time they were staying at the Sunny Days Bed & Breakfast with their parents. They had attended the Summer Friends Camp on their first day, and were excited to learn that the teenage girls who ran it, Ginny and Jen, were also best friends. Today was their second day of vacation, and they were both looking forward to finding out what Ginny and Jen had planned.

The tent was already ringing with laughter. Oscar and Lara, who they had met the previous day, were practicing one-handed cartwheels. When they collapsed to the ground, out of breath and giggling, Rachel and Kirsty came over to join them.

"Good morning!" said Lara in a cheerful voice. "It's great to see you here again. We're really looking forward to today."

"We are, too," said Kirsty. "We were just wondering what we'll be doing."

"Wonder no more!" said Ginny's friendly voice behind them. "We have something really awesome planned for today."

The children looked around and saw Ginny and Jen standing in the tent entrance, arm

in arm. Several other children crowded around them.

"We're going to paint a mural on the tennis clubhouse," said Jen, giving a little hop of excitement. "I'm so thrilled that we have the chance to do this. I know you're all super-creative, and we're going to make the best mural ever."

Chattering and giggling, Rachel and Kirsty headed across the park with the others. The clubhouse stood at the entrance to the tennis courts, and Jen and Ginny led everyone around to the back. They saw a small picnic area on a wooden deck, and Jen pointed at the long side wall of the clubhouse.

"This is the wall we're going to paint," she said. "They want us to brighten up the picnic area."

"What are we going to paint?" asked Oscar.

"The theme of the mural is friendship," said Ginny. "We thought that we could start by painting the word *friendship* on the wall. Then we can decorate it."

Jen took out a big book filled with letters and patterns.

"This book has tons of ideas for lettering styles and decorations for the mural," she said.

She handed the book to Oscar while Ginny passed out painting aprons. Kirsty and Rachel exchanged a big smile.

"A friendship mural," said Rachel in a low voice. "That's perfect."

"I can't wait to get started," said Kirsty.

Ginny and Jen went to get the paints and brushes from a shed at the side of the picnic area, and Rachel and Kirsty put on their painting aprons.

But suddenly, Kirsty felt someone tugging at her apron. She turned and saw a girl named Amy frowning at her.

"You got the best apron," said Amy. "It's not fair!"

Kirsty looked down at her apron in confusion.

"But mine's exactly the same as yours," she said.

"I want the one you're wearing!" said Amy.

Shrugging, and wanting to keep the peace, Kirsty handed her apron to Amy and picked up another one. Amy glared at her.

8

"You're keeping all the best ones for yourself!" she exclaimed. "That's mean."

"Kirsty is *not* mean!" Rachel cried, stepping forward to defend her friend.

But Amy had already turned away to argue about aprons with someone else.

Rachel and Kirsty went over to the picnic table, where Oscar was poring over the book of ideas.

"Could we have a look, too?" asked Rachel.

"Wait your turn," muttered Oscar.

Rachel and Kirsty looked at each other. Why were the other children suddenly being so selfish?

Fracturing Friendships

Suddenly, Oscar cried out. A boy named Eric had snatched the book from him.

"Give it back!" Oscar yelled.

"You're not sharing!" Eric retorted. "It's my turn now."

Just then, Jen and Ginny came back, their arms filled with paintbrushes and cans of paint.

"Now we can get started with the best part: painting!" said Kirsty.

But no one heard her—they were too busy arguing.

"Stop taking all the good brushes!" Amy was saying at the top of her voice. "*I* should get the best ones."

"I want the green paint," said Lara.

"No, *I* want it!" Eric yelled, grabbing the can of paint and trying to wrestle it away from Lara.

Meanwhile, Oscar had already started painting and had almost finished the *f* of the word *friendship* in red.

"Wait!" Amy wailed. "That's not fair! *Everyone* was supposed to help write the word. *I* wanted to write the *f.* I wanted to do it in purple!"

"Sorry," said Oscar. "You can all help me finish it."

Kirsty and Rachel joined him and started to paint.

"Hey!" said Lara. "Oscar is *my* best friend, so he should paint with *me*, not you!"

She glared at Kirsty and Rachel and dragged Oscar away from them. The girls looked at Ginny and Jen, hoping that they would break the fighting up. But the teenagers weren't looking at the children. They were each holding on tight to one end of a tennis racket, and they were both red in the face.

"I should have the racket," said Ginny. "The Rainspell Park Committee gave it as a thank-you for painting the wall, and painting it was my idea."

"No, it wasn't!" Jen exclaimed. "I thought of it first, and I was the one who got permission from the Park Committee, so *I* should get the tennis racket."

"But I organized getting all the paints and supplies," Ginny said through gritted teeth. "This racket should be mine."

Kirsty and Rachel exchanged a worried glance.

"I can't believe that they're fighting like this," said Rachel. "They're supposed to be best friends."

Kirsty looked around at the other children. They were all arguing now. Even Oscar and Lara were snatching paintbrushes out of each other's hands.

"Nobody wants to share anything," Kirsty said. "This is all because of Jack Frost and his troublesome goblins. None of them understands what true friendship is."

Jack Frost's troublemaking ways were fresh in their memories. Just the day before, the Friendship Fairies had invited Rachel and Kirsty to a tea party in Fairyland. The girls had been having a lovely time with Esther the Kindness Fairy, Mary the Sharing Fairy, Mimi the Laughter Fairy, and Clare the Caring Fairy—until Jack Frost and the goblins had snuck into the garden and stolen their magical objects!

Jack Frost had taken the magical objects so that he could be super-powerful and have lots of friends to boss around. He had ordered the goblins to take the magical objects to the human world and find some friends for him.

Remembering the shocked faces of the Friendship Fairies, Rachel felt more determined than ever to get the magical objects back.

"All these friendships should be strong and happy," she said, looking around at the other children. "Without the magical objects, they're all going to be ruined. We have to help all the Friendship Fairies get their objects back."

Watching Ginny and Jen, Kirsty felt tears of sympathy prickling her eyes. She thought about how horrible it would feel to argue with Rachel like that. Luckily, their old friend Florence the Friendship Fairy had cast a "Friends through Thick and Thin" spell on their bracelets, so their friendship wouldn't be affected. But

Florence's spell wouldn't last forever. If the fairies didn't get their magical objects back soon, even Rachel and Kirsty would turn against each other.

Rachel guessed what Kirsty was thinking and squeezed her hand.

"We helped Esther the Kindness Fairy get her magical heart brooch back from the goblins yesterday," she said. "We can do this—don't worry."

"It just seems like such a huge task," said Kirsty. "If we don't find the three remaining missing magical objects, *all* friendships will be ruined. People can't fight about every little thing and then still end up best friends."

Suddenly, there was a yell from the children beside the picnic table. Amy and Eric were covered in orange paint, which was also spilling all over the deck.

"That was your fault!" Amy snapped.

"No, you spilled it," Eric replied.

"Things are getting worse," said Rachel with a groan. "This is awful!"

Magic in a Mop Bucket

Jen and Ginny were so involved in their argument over the tennis racket that they hadn't noticed the paint spills.

"Let's go get a mop and bucket," said Rachel. "I don't think anyone else is going to clean it up. They're too busy arguing."

The girls made their way over to the shed and stepped inside. It took their eyes a few moments to adjust to being out of the bright sunshine. Then Rachel pointed to a far corner.

"There's a bucket," she said. "And there's a mop sticking out of it."

Kirsty stepped forward and picked up the mop. Suddenly, there was a tiny burst of sparkles, and Mary the Sharing Fairy fluttered out of the mop bucket.

Mary was wearing white skinny jeans, sparkly gold sandals, and a ruffly pink T-shirt with a patterned edge. The charm bracelets around her wrist rattled as she waved at the girls, but they knew that the most important charm of all was missing.

"Hello, Rachel and Kirsty!" Mary said eagerly. "I'm so happy that you came in here. I'm determined to find my magical yin-yang charm today, and I'm hoping that you might be able to help me."

23

"Of course we'll help you," said Kirsty. "We've just seen how horrible things are when friends don't share. It's spoiling everything that Jen and Ginny had planned."

Mary shook back her loose blond hair and her eyes sparkled behind her glasses.

"I'm sure that by working together, we'll be able to get the charm back," she said. "I believe that sharing really matters—and that means sharing trouble as well as sharing fun. With you two to help me, how can we fail?"

Rachel was remembering the tiny black-and-white charm that she had seen dangling from Mary's wrist when they first met.

"What does the yin and yang symbol mean?" she asked.

24

"Yin and yang are two opposite halves that make a whole when you put them together," said Mary.

"Just like friends," said Kirsty with a smile. "When two people work together, they can make a whole, true friendship."

"Exactly right," Mary replied. "Now, all three of us need to work together to find the missing charm and help people be able to share again. Let's go!"

Mary flew into the pocket of Kirsty's painting apron, and then the girls left the shed, carrying the mop and bucket.

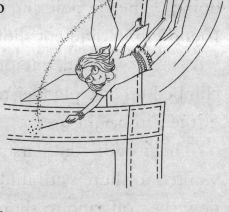

There was no one on the deck now—
the children were all crowded around the
mural.

As Rachel and Kirsty cleaned up the
spilled paint, they saw that a new group
of boys was standing among the other
children in the Summer Friends Camp.
They were all wearing green aprons and
matching hats.

"Look," said Rachel, standing up on
tiptoe to see what the new boys were
doing. "They're painting the *f* of
friendship in different shades of green."

As they watched, one of the boys
climbed up a stepladder to paint the top
of the *f* in bright green.

"That's odd," said Kirsty. "Amy hasn't
wanted to share with anyone else, but
now she's offering to share her purple

paint with that boy on the ladder.
The others are holding up their paints,
too."

Rachel and Kirsty walked closer to the
others, just as the boy on the ladder blew
a raspberry at Amy.

"We only like using green paint," he snapped. "Take that yucky purple away."

Rachel drew in her breath sharply. Under the boy's green hat, she caught a glimpse of a long green nose.

"Those aren't boys," she said to Kirsty in a low voice. "They're goblins! They must have Mary's magical object."

"But which one of them has it?" Kirsty asked.

"It must be the one on the ladder," said Rachel. "Everyone wants to share with him."

Just then, Jen handed the goblin another can of green paint.

"How about painting the rest of the mural in a different color?" she suggested.

The goblin simply grunted at her. Jen sent the other children to work farther down the wall on the rest of the mural. They all still seemed more interested in arguing than in painting, but for now they weren't paying attention to the goblins.

"I have an idea!" said Rachel.

Tennis Trouble

Rachel leaned down to whisper into the pocket of Kirsty's apron. "Mary, could you use your magic to change the color of the paint in the goblins' cans?" she asked.

She couldn't even see the little fairy, but then Mary poked out of the top of the pocket, and the girls heard her

31

silvery voice speaking the words of
a spell.

"Rainbow Fairies, hear my plea,
Lend your color spells to me.
Change the paint before their eyes
To a color they despise."

Mary's wand tip
waved, a
flash of
rainbow
sparkles
burst from
it, and in
an instant
the green
paint that the
goblins were
using turned
bright pink!

"Argh!" shouted the goblin on the ladder. "Disgusting! Give me a new can of paint!"

One of the goblins opened another green can, but the paint inside was also bright pink.

"This is ridiculous!" the goblin on the ladder squawked. "What's wrong with this paint?"

Kirsty and Rachel stepped forward.

"Nothing's wrong with it," said Kirsty. "You can have the green paint back as soon as you return Mary's magical charm. All you have to do is give back something that doesn't belong to you in the first place."

"It's the right thing to do," Rachel added seriously.

But the goblins curled their lips,
narrowed their eyes, and wrinkled
up their noses as if they had smelled
something bad.

"There's no way you're getting this
back," said the goblin on the ladder. He
held up his arm and jingled
the bracelet he was
wearing. Mary's
yin-yang charm was
dangling from it.

"It's mine now,
and I'm keeping it,"
he added. "Now leave
us alone!"

With that, the goblin jumped down
from the ladder and raced off toward
the tennis courts, closely followed by the
other goblins.

"It'll be easier to follow them as fairies,"
said Rachel. "Mary, will you use your
magic to transform us both?"

"Of course!" said Mary.

The girls darted around the corner
of the clubhouse, out of sight of the
other children. Then Mary popped out
of Kirsty's apron pocket and hovered in
front of them, holding her wand high
above her head.

"We have to save my yin-yang charm
Before more friendships suffer harm.
Untie these painting apron strings,
And lend my friends their fairy wings!"

Rachel and Kirsty felt something
magically pulling at them, and then the
aprons they were wearing were whisked
away. In the twinkling of an eye they
had shrunk into tiny fairies, their wings

shimmering like mother-of-pearl as they
rose into the air beside Mary.

"They're heading toward the tennis
courts," said Kirsty. "Come on, let's follow
them."

Two people were playing a tennis
match when the goblins ran onto the
court. One of the players was distracted
by them and hit the ball out-of-bounds,
but she didn't seem to mind. Instead, she
jogged over to the goblin with the yin-
yang charm and handed him her racket.

"Would you like to play now?" she asked him. "It only seems fair that we share so that you get a turn, too."

The goblin snatched the racket from her without saying thank you, while the other goblins argued over the second player's racket. The two players walked off toward the clubhouse.

The goblin with the charm picked up a tennis ball and threw it into the air a couple of times, catching it as it came down. He looked around and saw the fairies hovering beside the net. A mean smile flickered around his mouth. Then he hit the ball at the fairies as hard as he could. Rachel, Kirsty, and Mary dove in opposite directions. Quick as a flash,

he launched another ball at them, and another, and another. The fairies dodged left and right—it was all they could do to stay safe and keep away from the speeding tennis balls.

"There's no way we can get close to the charm while he's hitting balls at us," said Mary, panting. "Maybe we should leave and try again later."

Kirsty shook her head, but before she could reply she saw another tennis ball heading directly toward her. She darted sideways to avoid it, but she wasn't looking where she was going. *Crash!* She flew straight into the net that divided the tennis court!

Goblin in a Spin

In a tangle of arms, legs, and wings, Kirsty struggled to free herself. Rachel zoomed down to help.

"Are you OK?" Rachel asked, giving her a hug.

"I'm fine," said Kirsty, bubbling with excitement. "This has given me an idea that I really think might work!"

She told Rachel and Mary her plan, and then the three of them took their positions. The other goblins were still arguing when Rachel and Kirsty flew toward the goblin with the charm.

"I don't think you can hit us with those tennis balls," said Rachel in a loud voice. "Your aim isn't good enough."

"My aim is perfect!" the goblin squeaked. "You'd better get out of the way or I'll flatten you both like pancakes!"

"Oh, no you won't," said Kirsty with a laugh. "You're not quick enough."

Carefully, so that the goblin didn't even realize it was happening, Rachel and Kirsty led him closer to the net. He flung more balls at them, but they dodged them all and laughed, until the goblin became so angry that his eyes nearly popped out of his head.

"Stay still!" he hissed, stepping even closer to the net.

Rachel glanced sideways and saw Mary hiding beside the net. The Sharing Fairy held up one finger, meaning that she needed the goblin to come just one step closer.

Rachel and Kirsty fluttered backward.

"I've seen tennis balls being hit much harder and faster than this," said Rachel.

With a yell of rage, the goblin took
another step forward. Then Mary waved
her wand, and the tennis net flung itself
into the air
and wound
around the goblin,
rolling him up in
it like a mummy.
Within seconds,
all that could
be seen of the
goblin were
his angry
face and his
enormous
feet.

"Grrr!" he said,
baring his teeth at the fairies. "Let me go,
you flying pests!"

"You know what we want," said Mary. "Give me my charm and I will let you go."

"I'll share some tennis balls with you," the goblin offered. "You can even use my racket."

"The charm," said Rachel, folding her arms across her chest.

"I'll let you *have* all the tennis balls!" the goblin exclaimed. "And you can *keep* both rackets!"

"None of those things are even yours to give away," said Kirsty. "Give us the charm and Mary will set you free."

"I don't believe you," the goblin said, looking grumpy.

"Kirsty and I never tell lies, and neither do the fairies," said Rachel. "You can trust us to keep our promises."

"You can take all the other goblins prisoner!" shouted the goblin, sounding desperate now. "You can lock them

in dungeons and feed them moldy
bread!"

"We don't have dungeons in Fairyland,
and I don't want prisoners," said Mary.
"There is only one thing I want—the
charm that you and Jack Frost stole from
me. Give it back, and things will return to
normal."

"What if I don't like 'normal'?" the
goblin wailed.

"Then change it," said Kirsty. "You
don't *have* to do everything that Jack
Frost says, you know."

The goblin closed his eyes and made
a horrible face. Then he opened his eyes
again.

"Fine," he said. "I guess you three don't
care how much trouble I'm going to get
into for this."

The fairies didn't reply, but they
watched as the goblin wriggled and
jiggled around. It wasn't easy, because
his arms were pressed tightly against his
sides, but at last there was a tinkling sound
as something fell out of the bottom of the
tennis-net wrap.

The fairies dove toward it and saw the precious yin-yang charm. The goblin had managed to unhook it.

"At last!" said Mary, picking up the charm, which shrank to fairy size. "Oh, I was starting to worry that I would never get it back!"

She hooked it to her bracelet and tapped the tennis net with her wand. Immediately, the net unwound itself at top speed, sending the goblin staggering dizzily across the tennis court toward the other goblins.

He crashed into them, and they all fell
down together like dominoes.

The tennis net returned to its usual
position, and the fairies saw the goblins
start to bite their fingernails.

"Jack Frost is going to be so angry with
us," said one.

"That's two magical objects that we've lost now," said another. "He'll be furious! What are we going to do?"

Making Amends

The goblins looked so worried that the fairies felt sorry for them. Mary waved her wand, and magical red and white sparkles erupted into the air like a fountain.

"Even if they steal and pout,
I don't like leaving people out.
For I believe it's only fair
That everyone has treats to share."

In front of the goblins' eyes, the red
sparkles tumbled into a large bowl and
became strawberries, while the white
sparkles became whipped cream. The
goblins were delighted! They forgot
their worries as they tucked into the
treat, gobbling so fast that bright red
strawberry juice trickled down their
chins.

Laughing, the fairies turned to one another and shared a big, happy hug.

"You two have been so amazing," Mary told Rachel and Kirsty. "I've heard about what good friends you are, of course, but you're even more wonderful than I could have imagined. You're just like my yin-yang charm—you belong together."

As they hugged, the girls felt themselves growing and their wings disappearing. Then they were back to their usual size, and Mary was hovering in front of them.

"Good-bye!" she said, waving and smiling at them. "I hope we'll meet again soon!"

She disappeared in a starry swoosh of fairy dust, and the girls reached for each other's hands.

"Come on!" said Rachel. "Let's go and see how the others are getting along now that the charm is back where it belongs."

They raced back to the wall at the
back of the tennis clubhouse and found
Ginny, Jen, and the children gazing sadly
at the mural. After all the arguments,
paint splashes, and goblin interference, the
wall was a mess.

"What are we going to do?" asked
Amy.

Eric bent down and
picked up the book
of ideas. It fell open
to a colorful
page, and a little
smile appeared
on his face.

"Look at this,
everyone," he said, holding out the book
so that they could all share it. "I think we
might be able to fix it if we try this."

"Oh yes, what a good idea!" said Ginny. "It might work really well with the idea on page fifty."

They turned to the right page and agreed on exactly what they would do. Then, working together and sharing the paint and paintbrushes between them, the children  repainted and decorated the word *friendship* on the wall. Kirsty painted one of the letters with Oscar, while Rachel painted with Lara.

"It's fun sharing friends, isn't it?" said Lara.

Rachel smiled back at her, feeling happy that Lara was back to her normal, friendly self.

While they painted, the girls noticed Ginny and Jen chatting about what to do with the tennis racket. They had been arguing about it earlier, but now they were full of smiles.

"You should have it, Ginny," said Jen. "You deserve it more than I do."

"No way," said Ginny. "It's all yours."

Kirsty grinned at Rachel and then leaned over to the teenagers.

"Why don't you share it?" she suggested. "You could take turns using it to play, or bouncing a tennis ball on it!"

They exchanged a glance and nodded.

"That's the perfect solution," said
Ginny. "Why didn't we think of it?"

Kirsty and Rachel knew why! But,
of course, they could never tell anyone
about their fairy adventures, so they just
shared a secret smile.

Later, when the mural was finished

and looked amazing, the children helped
Ginny and Jen clean all the brushes and
put away the cans of paint. It was hot
working in the sunshine, but everyone
was glad to help.

Rachel and Kirsty said good-bye to
the others and headed back to the bed
and breakfast. On the way, they passed
the Rainspell Island ice cream stand,
which was run by a friendly lady named
Heather.

"Are you thinking what I'm thinking?"
Rachel asked her best friend with a grin.

"Definitely!" said Kirsty.

They bought an ice cream cone to
share and took turns licking it as they
walked along.

"Sharing is something we do all the
time as best friends," said Rachel as

Kirsty caught a drip of strawberry ice cream with her tongue. "I'm so glad that we found Mary's magical charm."

"Me, too," said Kirsty, handing the cone to Rachel. "Now all friends will remember to share. But friendships aren't quite safe yet. We have to find the two other missing magical objects for the Friendship Fairies. I hope we get the chance to help them very soon."

"Tomorrow is a brand-new day," said Rachel, smiling at Kirsty. "And I'm sure that it'll bring us a brand-new adventure with our fairy friends!"

Rachel and Kirsty found Esther's
and Mary's missing magic items. Now it's
time for them to help

Mimi
the Laughter Fairy!

Join their next adventure in this
special sneak peek . . .

Mr. Twinkle's Tumble

Kirsty Tate was spinning her way across the park, her arms outstretched as she soaked up the early morning sunshine. It was making the dew sparkle on each blade of grass, and it was shining on the golden hair of Kirsty's best friend, Rachel Walker.

"I wonder what Jen and Ginny have planned for us today," said Rachel, skipping along beside Kirsty.

It was their third day on Rainspell Island, the beautiful place where they had first met—and where they'd had their first fairy adventure! They were attending the Summer Friends Camp, a day camp for children staying on the island on vacation. The camp was held in the park every morning.

"We've already played soccer, had a water-balloon fight, and painted a mural," Kirsty remembered. "I'm so glad we've been going to camp."

They reached the tent where the camp was based and stepped inside. Oscar and Lara, two of their newest friends, dashed over to them.

"Good morning!" said Lara, a big smile on her face.

"Do you know what we're doing today?" Oscar asked.

"We have no idea," said Rachel with a grin. "But I think we're about to find out!"

Jen and Ginny, the teenage best friends who ran the camp, were beckoning everyone to gather around them. They looked as if they were about to burst with excitement.

"Today we have something really fantastic for you all to enjoy," said Ginny. "We're going to watch a special performance by Mr. Twinkle himself!"

Everyone gasped and squealed. Mr. Twinkle was the funniest, most famous magician on TV. Like all the others at the camp, Rachel and Kirsty watched his show every week.

"I can't believe we're actually going to see him *in real life*!" Oscar said in a breathless voice. "When I grow up, I want to be just like him and make everyone laugh!"

"Where's the performance going to be held?" Kirsty asked.

"Right here in Rainspell Park," said Jen with a smile. "We have to wait for him on the steps of the fountain square. I thought you could all race one another to see who gets there first. Ready? Set? Go!"

Everyone sped out of the tent and sprinted across the grass to the fountain in the middle of the park. A girl named Anouk won the race, and everyone gathered around to congratulate her.

RAINBOW magic

Which Magical Fairies Have You Met?

- ❑ The Rainbow Fairies
- ❑ The Weather Fairies
- ❑ The Jewel Fairies
- ❑ The Pet Fairies
- ❑ The Sports Fairies
- ❑ The Ocean Fairies
- ❑ The Princess Fairies
- ❑ The Superstar Fairies
- ❑ The Fashion Fairies
- ❑ The Sugar & Spice Fairies
- ❑ The Earth Fairies
- ❑ The Magical Crafts Fairies
- ❑ The Baby Animal Rescue Fairies
- ❑ The Fairy Tale Fairies
- ❑ The School Day Fairies
- ❑ The Storybook Fairies
- ❑ The Friendship Fairies

SCHOLASTIC

HiT entertainment

Find all of your favorite fairy friends at
scholastic.com/rainbowmagic

RMFAIRY17

RAINBOW magic™

SPECIAL EDITION

Which Magical Fairies Have You Met?

❑ Joy the Summer Vacation Fairy
❑ Holly the Christmas Fairy
❑ Kylie the Carnival Fairy
❑ Stella the Star Fairy
❑ Shannon the Ocean Fairy
❑ Trixie the Halloween Fairy
❑ Gabriella the Snow Kingdom Fairy
❑ Juliet the Valentine Fairy
❑ Mia the Bridesmaid Fairy
❑ Flora the Dress-Up Fairy
❑ Paige the Christmas Play Fairy
❑ Emma the Easter Fairy
❑ Cara the Camp Fairy
❑ Destiny the Rock Star Fairy
❑ Belle the Birthday Fairy
❑ Olympia the Games Fairy
❑ Selena the Sleepover Fairy

❑ Cheryl the Christmas Tree Fairy
❑ Florence the Friendship Fairy
❑ Lindsay the Luck Fairy
❑ Brianna the Tooth Fairy
❑ Autumn the Falling Leaves Fairy
❑ Keira the Movie Star Fairy
❑ Addison the April Fool's Day Fairy
❑ Bailey the Babysitter Fairy
❑ Natalie the Christmas Stocking Fairy
❑ Lila and Myla the Twins Fairies
❑ Chelsea the Congratulations Fairy
❑ Carly the School Fairy
❑ Angelica the Angel Fairy
❑ Blossom the Flower Girl Fairy
❑ Skyler the Fireworks Fairy
❑ Giselle the Christmas Ballet Fairy
❑ Alicia the Snow Queen Fairy

■ SCHOLASTIC

Find all of your favorite fairy friends at
scholastic.com/rainbowmagic

3 stories in each one!

HiT entertainment

RMSPECIAL20